Blueskin
The Cat

Blueskin The Cat

FootSteps Press First Edition

Typeset by Jackie Pascoe

ISBN 978-0-9566349-3-1

In this work of Fiction the characters, places
and events are either the product of the author's
imagination of they are used entirely fictitiously.
Therefore any resemblance to Persons living or
dead is coincidental.

Except for the pirates who are known personally to
the writer and are a pretty rotten lot.

Blueskin
The Cat

by

Daniel Nanavati

water-colours by

Gabriela Sepulveda

To All Cats

Chapters

Blueskin and the King of the Netherlands

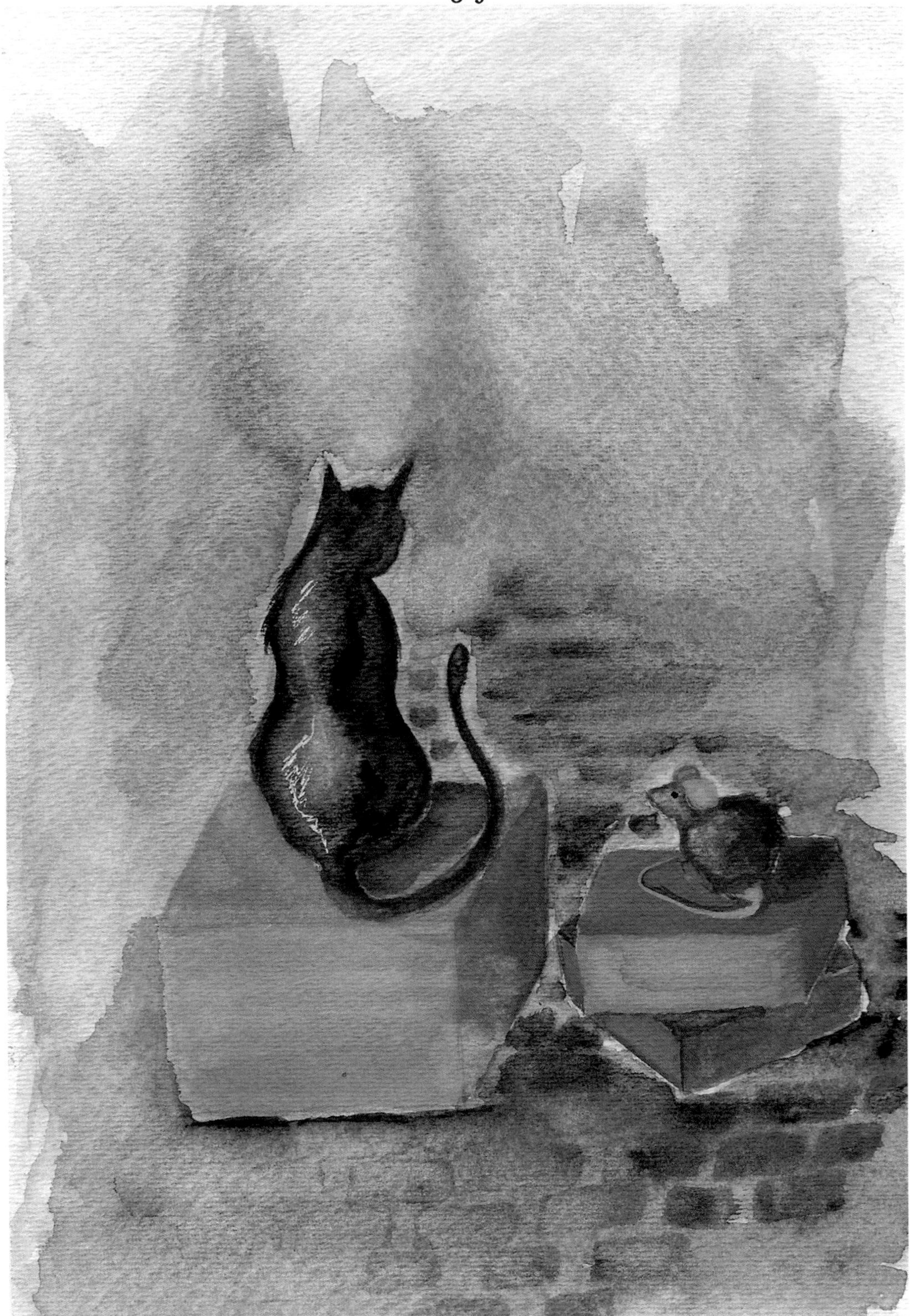

The Cat

Blueskin wasn't bothered by thoughts of an after-life. He couldn't spell reincarnation and hadn't even heard of India where the people believed in such things.

What did bother him for a moment was the awful memory of being strangled to death in a hanging and the loss of his beautiful, blue waistcoat with the pearl buttons that had been his pride and joy as a highwayman. He remembered the sound of the drum roll and a great cheer from the crowd as his body dropped and the rope tightened around his neck.

He looked down at his chest and was even more bothered to see fur had grown all over him.

Fur?

Black fur with a definite blue sheen?

One, two, three, four paws?

Paws?

His chin was touching the dirty floor. He must be lying on his stomach. He glanced around at the casks lining the walls, wooden boxes stacked on top of each other and coal in a large pile. This was a cellar. How had he fallen into a cellar from the scaffold? Had they carried him in here and dumped him on his stomach ready to be carted away to the lime grave as soon as they were ready? He had fooled them. He was still alive. He could still move. He stretched his neck. It didn't hurt. He tried to smile and felt fur on his lips. Something was wrong. The military had hanged too many men to make a mistake.

There were smells in the air he didn't recognize. Things he had never smelled before. He licked his nose which he had never been able to do before. He turned round very slowly and watched with fascination as a tail flicked. A cat's tail. His tail.

His tail!

He was a cat!

A blue-black cat. He scratched his stomach where it itched with his back leg. He sat down and looked at his rump. He could turn his head almost right round. He could see quite well in the dark and heard a few mice scuttling across the stone floor of the cellar. Muscles all over him tensed at their every movement. His mouth filled with saliva when he smelled them and he felt his claws aching to come out and grab them.

He wanted to eat them!

What a ghastly, terrible, catastrophic twist of fate! He jumped onto a box and leapt in a single bound onto the ledge of the barred window. Now he was at street level and could see ladies' petticoats and men's buckled shoes milling around in the square. Gaps appeared in their ranks and suddenly he saw his scaffold! The pads of his front paw lightly touched the bars in his shock.

There it was. His blue waistcoat being auctioned even as his body was dumped into the open cart.

"What am I bid for this infamous coat," called the hangman who doubled as an auctioneer,

"Marv'lous workminship. Six purl buttons. Worth two pounds of money and a right good piece for conversation. Make the ladies' blood run cold an' ready for an 'ug! Sixpence. Be reason'ble 'e was wearing this the day 'e killed Lord Duncan. Look it's a bit o' a celebration the roads being that bit cleaner and safer an' all. Let's 'ave one pound ten shillings? One pound? Come on. This 'ere's a piece o' 'istory. 'Is bounty was two 'undred pound. Worn on the day 'e died and went to 'ell. Fifteen and six? Sold!"

Then his horse was brought forward and he saw the rich amongst the crowd going over to it to see if it was worth a few gold coins. His grey stallion. Gone for ten pounds seven and sixpence.

"Meow!" He sat down. He had wanted to bellow out, "Stop!" but instead out came a meow. A cat's sound. He really was a cat. He stood up and turned round again. How had this happened? Why had this happened? If he had been offered the choice he'd have preferred Hell to this!

He remembered the night before. The four drunken soldiers who had chased him. The feel of the precious necklace in his greedy fingers, the scent of the lace 'kerchiefs. He curled his claws and they scrapped at the stone ledge as he remembered the two brothers who has captured him just after he had given the soldiers the slip. He opened his black eyes as a jeer went up. Someone was holding up the trousers he had been wearing. They'll sell anything to make some money to pay for the hanging. The crowd spat at his body on its way to be quicklimed.

But he was still alive.

He was a live cat.

Wasn't that better than being dead. He heard the mice again and his stomach did a somersault.

UGH! The thought of it.

After he had poached venison, eaten chicken, ham and eggs, rabbits and beef pies, to be brought down to mice! Little brown, dirty common mice. Yet how crunchy they would be.

After being a man to be brought down to being a cat! He used to kick cats. Worse he had enjoyed kicking cats. He inflicted the maximum pain at twenty paces to a cat of any size with his expert choice of stones.

He looked down at himself. He was an above average size blue-black cat. At least he still had something blue about his person. He peered at his backside. He was a tom cat. At least that hadn't changed.

The crowd had begun to disperse and he realised he had thought so much about himself he had missed the price they had raised for his belongings. His? They weren't his anymore. The waistcoat would hardly fit a cat, even a vain cat of above average size had little use for a waistcoat with pearl buttons. He flicked his tail and watched his coffined, old body being driven to be dumped and forgotten forever. Well, maybe not forever since he was now a cat maybe he would be a man once again one day and ...

He was now a cat!

Blood pounded in his small brain at the thought. No more riding across the highways. No more kissing women in keeper Filyrank's inn. No more robbery with violence, drinking with other men until he couldn't stand up straight. No more fighting with his fists and using bad language.

No more rich and tasty meals followed by wines of the finest vintages bought with the sale of other people's best jewels. All that was being carted away with the two men sent to see his body legally disposed of as the colonel in chief had ordered. All he had to look forward to was eating mice and rats and helping she cats have kittens.

What kind of a life was that for an adventurous, tough and hardy highwayman!

He felt cold and bedraggled. He didn't even have a name anymore. He didn't have a home...well he had never had a home so that wouldn't make much difference. He didn't have a horse. Who had his horse. He looked up but whomever had bought his horse had gone. He wasn't feared by travellers any more; wasn't respected by robbers and thieves; wasn't hunted by soldiers. He was just a cat. To all intents and purposes he was dead.

He had an awful feeling life as a cat was going to be boring.

Why hadn't anyone ever told him if he died he might become a cat? Maybe no one he had talked to knew? Maybe it was only hanged highwaymen who became cats. No, there are too few highwaymen and too many cats for that to be true. Maybe not all cats have been people? He flicked his tail. At least he could still remember even if he could only mew. His stomach tightened. He had to eat. To eat, sleep and decide what to do. If there was anything to do. He decided to make his way to the market and see if he could pick up a few scraps of old food.

'You're new around here,' observed a voice. Blueskin turned and saw a mouse sitting on one of the boxes below him.

'Who are you?'

'Now? A mouse, but once I was King of the Netherlands.'

'You too?'

'I'm afraid so. I've been running around for ten minutes and you haven't moved a muscle. That's a sure sign you're new to this game.'

'I ... I never thought of it,' lied Blueskin restraining his desire to leap onto the poor rodent.

'I know how you feel. Imagine me. I had servants, carriages, palaces and lots of food and these days I have to get used to cellars, pantry scraps and avoiding cats.'

'Is it hard?'

'To begin with. How are you finding it?'

'I'm...confused.'

'Always the way of things. What were you?'

'I was called Blueskin.'

'My! That's a quick one. You've only just been hanged.'

'You saw?'

'I like to see what's happening in the square.'

'Does this sort of thing usually take longer?'

'I didn't turn up for a week. I met a mole once who didn't make an appearance for a whole year after being a sheriff.'

Blueskin looked down

'I never thought anything like this would happen.'

'None of us do. I've met two rats who wanted to commit suicide over it but once they realised how the system worked they decided to stay as rats. No telling where they'd end up being next. A real shock to the old mind I can tell you.'

'It certainly is,' agreed Blueskin.

'Well I wish you luck. I just thought I'd tell you aren't alone. It might help.'

'Thank you ... your highness.' The mouse twitched its whiskers.

'Thanks for that,' it ended and slipped away.

Blueskin left the ledge and walked across the square very much as he would have done if he had been a man. Except he was wondering just how long cats lived instead of wondering when the next coach was due.

His eyes watered at the foul smell of urine mixed with the mud which didn't leave the cobbled streets until it rained. No one knew about sewers and still less about street cleaning. His feet stank! No wonder cats walked about with their heads in the air, the smell was unbearable! As he was dawdling a girl pulled at his tail and he flew up in fright and pain spitting as if he had been spitting all his life only to receive a stone in his side thrown from a black-toothed, ugly boy standing nearby!

There was laughter and a hail of other stones as Blueskin turned and ran into an alley. His side was sore, his pride hurt and his mind angry. People shouldn't be so cruel! Ignorant! Hurtful!

He stopped himself.

He had done the same. Was he superior now he was a cat? Yes! He wiggled his body gently. He had better get to the market. He carried on, only now he was slinking stealthily along the walls keeping a sharp look-out for groups of children glad his body was very lithe. He wasn't so hurt.

The market was doing poor business. Stalls were half-stocked as farmers were having to bring the food in with fewer workers every day. Plague was claiming many lives. Nevertheless Blueskin could see quite a few decent scraps about the place which might be appetizing. The only problem was every other cat and most of the dogs in the town saw the same scraps. They were all fighting furiously beneath the stalls and around the people in a chaos of fur, claws, barks and bites. If you think a food-fight means custard pies and lemonade over your best friend forget it! A food fight means being a cat facing a dog over a hog's foot and blood being shed.

Blueskin had been reincarnated with movements only a cat can perform. How to scratch a dog on the nose where its softest, flick the tail to distract its attention whilst you get a claw or two in position, twist before another dog bites your back and jump with claws extended and scratch whilst running away.

Each and every one of which he used in the first minute it took to collect a piece of rotting fish from the bin beside the fish seller. He wanted some fresh fish but the man at the counter was using a fierce looking axe to keep away animals and thieves.

Blueskin crept along the back of the market whilst people called out their wares and swore at urchins who stole an apple here, a choice vegetable there. He could smell a faint aroma of cooked meat probably coming from the officers' quarters at the end of the square. The soldiers knew how to eat and officers had plenty of money.

He stopped for a moment in surprise.

Ahead of him he could see one of the two brothers who had saluted him as he was being hanged. One of the two men who had caught him the night before. For a moment thoughts of revenge fled into his mind and he reached down for his pistol but he ended up scratching himself. He spat. How can an angry cat avenge itself on a human being? It didn't seem possible.

Then again Blueskin wasn't the kind to give up easily once he had decided upon something whatever he was! He swallowed his piece of fish, avoided the hostile attentions of a male cat covered in scars and licking away the blood of some dog's nose from its claws. Blueskin ran to the far end of the square where the man was talking and placed himself close to his boots.

"That's right. I was one of them. A close thing it was too. My associate in the business and brother has a cut across the back of his shooting hand to prove it." Blueskin recognised the voice of the man who had jumped on him from the trees.

"It was a fine job though a dangerous one," responded the old baker he was talking too. "Needed doing and the military weren't too hot on his trail. Well worth the two hundred to be rid of him."

"Dark it was. He rode up right under the tree but it was

a near thing. Still there were no dangers we hadn't expected. We tracked that highwayman for three weeks since his robbing of Lord St.John Thackery. Slept out most nights but we got the fox in the end. Though he was more like a cat with his wiles and craftiness. I've never seen a shot like it. Pitch black and it went straight as an arrow taking the pistol right out of my brother's hand. We made him walk all the way into town to take the wind out of him."

"There was talk he came from another place," said the old man in a hushed whisper suggesting Blueskin was a devil.

"There was nothing like that about him. He didn't change into an animal or disappear into a mist. And that neck was as leathery and human as yours or mine," he grinned. "Nay he wasn't a devil. Far from it, a man like that could have been one of the best shots in England. Perhaps the best, mark my words."

"Well that's as that is. Now he's dead and we'll get on better without him."

"That you will. Thank you kindly for the bread old man. How much is it?"

"One and half-penny."

"Take two pence and welcome to it."

He stopped talking and looked down as a cat rubbed its

blue-black back against his foot.

"Scab! Get out!" cried the old man picking up a stone from a pile he kept for just such use.

"Leave it old man. It's a hungry cat. You've got quite a few here."

"Pah! Its always the same. Like peasants they breed and breed and little else. We're still infested with rats and mice despite the lot of 'em. Useless mangy animals."

He put the stone back not wishing to offend a customer.

"Well a little good fortune can stretch from man to beast can it not. Let me have some of that cheese."

The man bent down and gave Blueskin some cheese which was almost like thick creamy milk. Blueskin licked his whiskers. Blueskin could make use of him whilst he planned his demise. After all he needed to eat and fighting other animals all the time would sap his strength. Besides now he had had the fortune to find one of his captors he wanted to track down the other one. He would be nice and follow this man to his lodgings and bide his time. Maybe he could get them both killed at the same time!

Things weren't going to be so boring after all.

John and Anthony

The Brothers

Blueskin, having been rotten most of his human life, didn't have the faintest idea that some cats get more spoilt than children. He didn't know people stroked them, fed them, cuddled them, confided in them, smiled at them and let them sit on their laps. Blueskin didn't know what it was to be picked up and cradled in someone's arms. He wasn't used to being tickled under his chin or having his ears rubbed. He would have been astonished to be kissed, hugged or groomed. Especially by a man. Luckily for Blueskin the brothers didn't like kissing cats.

The man talked to Blueskin as they walked away from the baker and passed the cathedral steps where most of the market was in progress. They went down the granite steps at the end of the square and along the streets which wound their way westward. The road was muddy and he had never thought about it before but now he wasn't wearing any boots he had to be very careful where he stepped or what he stepped in.

'People were really, really mucky creatures,' he thought.

"Well, well my beauty. Coming with me eh?" he said looking at Blueskin with one eye.

"Is it because of the cheese? If it is you may as well know I can't go giving you good food all the time. I can't hardly afford enough for one let alone two."

Blueskin flicked his tail.

'Rubbish!' He thought and gave an outraged meow. 'Not enough for one! Half a share in the reward was a hundred pounds in gold. A man and a cat could live happily on that for two years if the inflation rate stays steady.' (A cat can get a great deal into one meow if they try.)

"Still," went on the man, "a cat must take its chances like any of us and where there's one meal there may yet be two, eh?" He whistled as he walked.

Blueskin had a definite aversion to this man who had helped to have him hanged. He didn't let that stop him from sticking to him like glue whilst they walked to his rendezvous. It wasn't that he was afraid of losing him. Far from it! His nose picked out the most awful smells none of which he had known before. He was finding out each person smelled different from any other. He could have followed his scent as well as a dog if he had wanted.

He was afraid of the ragamuffins and their stones. He

wondered how many cats had walked in dread of him in the days he was able to walk around a town without being recognized. There was no fear of being recognized now but he could be hit by a stone, snatched and skinned by some hungry, ugly murderer or have dogs set on him for the fun of it. He felt very vulnerable. He looked at everyone's faces as he passed them.

That smile could be a leer!

Why is he licking his lips? Is he tasting me before he has me in a pot and cooked?

Why is that one fingering a knife? Does he know how to skin a cat?

Do they think I'm a witch in disguise? (He knew all about how they strung cats up in bags and beat them.)

Blueskin kept pace with the man deciding that anyone, even his captor, was preferable to this town's horrid and frightening inhabitants.

Eventually they arrived at the inn in which the man was staying. Blueskin was still no more than an inch away from the man's foot. A fire roared merrily in the open grate, beer was served with a meal and in every corner men sat calling to the serving maids for more than the bill. A wave of remembrance passed through Blueskin and made him feel warm all over.

The man stood by the fire for a moment to warm his hands and then sat near the window with Blueskin curled around his feet. Blueskin didn't want to curl up but he found it was comfortable and although he hadn't noticed it outside, he suddenly felt shivery and grateful for the fire. Whether it was the cold or his strange predicament he didn't know but he was almost asleep in five minutes. Then his other captor came in, sat opposite his brother and accidentally kicked Blueskin who was under the table.

The cat meowed and jumped up onto the table and then onto the window sill staring at the man fiercely with raised hackles and arched body. The man's mouth dropped open as the fire light caught the blue sheen on the cat's coat.

"By the saints!" He crossed himself and spat on the ground.

"What? Oh, the cat. It hasn't left me since I gave it a bit of cheese at the market."

"'Tis blue amidst its black! 'Tis an omen!"

"Of what?" scoffed the other man, "Trust you to come up with some notion or other. Hardly what I have waited to see you for!"

"Anthony mock me not! This may be devil's work! Not two hours dead and a cat appears to you bearing his mark! That's no tiding I care to meet with"

"Not two hours dead and you're seeing ghosts!" mocked Anthony. "Come, John give me the news. What did she say?"

"Anthony it may not be wise to speak with this creature listening?"

"Wisdom isn't my strong point, John, and this cat was hungry. That's all."

"Nay I trust it not!"

"For heavens sake!"

"Ay, you do right to call on Heaven. Perhaps there is the power to help us."

"John, pull yourself together and tell me what she said before I thump you!" John looked at Anthony and then at the cat,

"Be it on your own head. I would rather not have spoken before such a one as this. I like it not. I cannot help you with your marriage."

"She won't have me."

"I didn't say that. She merely hit me and said she wanted a man who would stand up to her father not one who sends his brother along. She said if you can capture Blueskin you can fight for her hand in marriage against anyone."

"She's right. I would feel the same way."

"Then fight him!"

"He's a better swordsman and marksman than I. That's why we decided I should grab Blueskin from behind. I'd never have held the pistol straight! If I faced her father I'd be killed and she would marry another. There must be another way."

"There is!"

"What? Tell me quickly! You have an idea?"

"Let's take the money we have and be off to the Americas. They say the land is rich and ready for the taking. We could build an empire with the two hundred pounds. I can get us passage aboard a galleon no less, for twenty pounds each, even less if we work and with my experience in the navy that should cut the cost by half."

"Call that an idea! I'd never stop thinking about her and by the time I could come back she'd have married someone else. I'll go with you but not without her!"

"You'll have to steal her before you get her to the altar."

"Why not? Do you think she'd come along if I went to her?"

"It seems to me that if you face her father he will kill you and if he finds you eloping he will kill you but at least eloping you have a chance of being together. She didn't say she'd reject you. In fact I think the woman loves you."

"Settled," said Anthony sitting back and finishing his

drink.

"We shall go tonight. Where does the galleon leave for the Americas?"

"Portsmouth."

"When?"

"Three days from now if winds be fair."

"Then let's hope the three of us will be on her!"

In the 1740s ale was a potent drink. Straight from a wooden barrel where it had fermented for months it goes down easily but hits you hard when you try to get up. It was rather unfortunate then that two slightly drunken brothers rose and made their unsteady way to their horses at the stable.

Blueskin decided to follow having had a sip or two from the table to remind him what being human was like. If he was going to get any revenge he thought he had better stay close. Besides he could never get to Portsmouth without them.

Once on their horses they rode slowly slightly swaying in their saddles, to a brick and wood house on the outskirts of town with very woozy heads and wild ideas. They arrived at a desirable residence by the river with a new innovation in the latest fashion, a garden of flowers. Still showing the remains of a moss lawn and violet strew paths of its Tudor past, it has seven rooms, hall, small library, three dangerous guard dogs, a stable, two main doors, and a long, winding track over which horses' hooves could be heard in the drawing room.

Heard by a young, impetuous girl called Matilda in love with a self-styled adventurer called Anthony who is slightly drunk and doesn't know it. She walked to the window and saw him riding up the pathway with John listing in his saddle beside him. She didn't notice the cat coming behind in the twilight the stars mirrored in his eyes.

Turning swiftly she ran to the front door, opened it and ran to meet them "Anthony! What are you doing here!"

Anthony slipped off his horse, crumpled to his knees and picked himself up with her help,

"I am going ... going to ... to ... what am I going to do, John?"

"Marry her," reminded John. He smiled as he remembered. The ale from the barrel had really got to him.

"That's it! With or without that ... old scoot's permission."

"Father will murder you!" she cried of the old scoot.

"Death or marriage!" he cried aloud.

'Some would think them the same,' thought Blueskin.

He walked slowly up to the door choosing where to put his paws very carefully. He looked around and sniffed the air.

Anthony tried to draw the sword he carried by his side. She held his arm back.

"Please, dearest, don't be rash."

"But I ... that is we thought ... you wanted me ... to come here!"

"I did."

"Well ... I'm here," he hiccupped, attempting to smile. "And what's more ... there's a boat leaving for the New World ... and we're going to ... going to ... what are we going to do, John?"

"Sail away to the Americas," said John waving from his horse in the general direction they would be taking.

'Let's see,' wondered Blueskin, 'With all this noise I give the old boy five full minutes to put down his port, reach the window, see what's going on, open it and ... '

"What's all that noise!" thundered a voice from the second floor.

Blueskin licked his whiskers. 'Right on time'.

"Blaggard! I told you to stay away from my daughter. I'll have you, you vagabond! Wait 'till I get down there. Walerts! Get the guns! Loose the dogs!" Walerts was the butler and dog-handler.

"Quickly, go!" she begged him, "He's gone to get his

blunderbuss. He'll blow you to pieces!"

"Not until ... until you consent to be my wife!"

"You know I love you!"

"Then let's go to the New World and be done. . .be done with your father and this life. John has ... has ... I forget but I know it's important. What have you got, John?"

'That's it. Keep talking. Oh! Am I going to enjoy this!' Thought Blueskin who gave them another thirty seconds.

"I've got berths on a galleon sailing for the Americas from Portsmouth next Tuesday!"

"I can't!" she moaned.

Blueskin sat down by the earthen pot of lavender. He had a good view and was eyeing up the likely places pieces of Anthony would fall when Matilda's father shot him.

"Ah!" Cried the father appearing at the door, "Damn you to Hell! Matilda get away from that man!"

"Father please!" she screamed protecting Anthony who couldn't quite see where her father was standing but was still prepared to fight the blunderbuss with his sword.

"Down or so help me I'll shoot the two of you where you stand!" bellowed her father turning red in high anger.

"But I love him!" she cried as her father aimed with the hammer cocked back.

'If he shoots him he'll die quickly enough I suppose,'

thought Blueskin. 'But I won't have killed him. On the other hand if we have to get rid of them one at a time maybe John should be the first. No, he wasn't the one who fell on me. That really hurt. They are each as bad as the other and it doesn't matter who gets it. It wouldn't be a bad idea if Matilda got it as well, stupid woman going crazy over Anthony. No accounting for taste!'

By now the woman was in tears and the cook and maid were watching with open eyes from the windows above. If they had had television it couldn't have been much better. This was the best soap in town. The father hesitated. Blueskin watched in amazement as he just stood there. Nothing was happening. Blueskin had not expected to have such a chance to get rid of either of them so quickly and he wasn't about to let them escape. It wasn't the slow, painful revenge he wanted but it was handy and would do the trick.

Blueskin sharpened his claws on the stones. The father still wavered in his resolve because after all, this was his daughter. The port was wearing off and the cold was getting to his bare feet. Blueskin eyed the thin dressing gown he was wearing and watched as he looked down his leveled blunderbuss, seeming unable to fire.

In one bound he attached himself to the father's rear and

dug in hoping to surprise him into action. It worked. The man cried out in fright, threw up his hands and fired the blunderbuss harmlessly into the air. Guttering went flying from the roof and the maid and cook screamed and dived under their beds. At the sound of the shot Anthony and John suddenly burst into action. Anthony grabbed Matilda and pushed her onto his horse madly trying to get on as well and wondering where he had been hit.

"I can't go," she argued.

"If we stay here we're ... we're ... what are we, John?"

"Dead I should say,"replied his brother making sure it wasn't he who had been hit.

"Come, to Portsmouth!" begged Anthony as he finally got hold of the reins. Blueskin ran towards them as Matilda's father got off the porch steps and ran inside for a sword, careering out with a whoop at a charge happily recalling his days in the army hoping to thrash the Russians who were making off with daughter,(the port hadn't worn off that much.)

'Damn it! The old scoot missed the lot of them!' Thought Blueskin.

As a last act Blueskin scratched his bare foot as he came out and sent him hopping into the rhododendron bush newly imported from China.

'That will teach him to be a terrible shot. Twenty paces and he missed. No right to own a gun! I don't know what they taught you in the army but I could have shot ten men in the time it took you to miss two!'

He ran to John's horse and jumped onto the saddle as Anthony and Matilda bolted on their mount down the road.

"You're a fine fighter, just like the ghost of Blueskin would have been," said John who was far too superstitious to push the cat off and actually thought the cat had tried to save them.

The father was still waving the sword whilst on his back in the bush as they rode away to Portsmouth and adventure on the high seas.

Blueskin wrapped himself in John's cloak. He had to go along with them even though he had never been much of a sailor. Still he might not have to wait for his revenge until they actually put to sea. No doubt this girl's father would inform the military his daughter had been kidnaped and they would be hunted down by teams of rampaging soldiers.

The idea appealed to Blueskin who felt really at home with three people on the run, two of whom were his sworn enemy in his last life. It was almost family.

This situation was developing nicely.

The Hope of the Seas

The Ship

When Anthony sobered up he had to get some travelling clothes for Matilda before Matilda decided to go travelling without him. And since they had spent an entire night in the same boarding house her honour was now impeached and she would have to marry him. It was the first thing Anthony heard the next morning,

"Oh! Anthony. You'll have to marry me now."

"As if there was any doubt about it!" he smiled.

"Well you were tipsy and I feared lest…"

"Lest nothing. We are as good as man and wife already!"

Which was of course exactly the best thing to say, and exactly the best thing to say is always the thing to say, as we all know.

Whilst Anthony was made to go round a few tailors to see what could be made in three days that fitted, John sent a courier by stagecoach to Portsmouth reserving the additional berth on the galleon 'Hope of the Seas', which he was told was a reasonable ship and not a bad galleon.

Blueskin went with him and spent an unpleasant day finding out how unpleasant mice, cockroaches and flies are to eat and how hard it is to stop a weevil crawling along a piece of wood even with quick paws because it kept sneaking in between the pads of his feet.

The men on the crowded quay were loading the ship to the tune of fiddlers who were standing beside them. They were singing as they went to help them forget they were tired of lifting half-tonne kegs aboard with manual lifting gear. In fact they had been loading the ship for a week and no one had been allowed any leave. Singing was their only pleasure.

♪ Heave! Ho! Americas,
That's where we will roam;
Heave! Ho! If going's fair
I'll leave a wench home;
Heave! Ho! A fairy-child
Waves us on the tide;
Heave! Ho! I don't know
Shall I stay or go;
Heavel Ho! Captain's back
There's no time to slack ♪

"Move yerselves!" bawled one of largest men Blueskin had ever seen with one of the largest hats sporting a very ancient ostrich feather given to him by a Dutchman he beat senseless at cards.

Obviously he made the decisions.

Blueskin jumped on a bail of straw being sent aloft to bed the goats, chickens, ducks and pigs aboard; fresh meat for the officers and captain. The animals made a great deal of noise as they were carried up the gang-plank or hoisted into the pens and strange to tell Blueskin almost thought he could understand some of them.

Blueskin sniffed at the packages and boxes. These were the men's provisions. They had to eat from the store of salted beef, pork and fish, dried biscuits (some 20,000 of them!) peas, suet and oatmeal. Oh yes and Blueskin smelled something else. Vinegar. Lots of it. Meant to flavour the salted meat once it had turned sour and stank. His stomach tightened and his eyes watered. How had he ever eaten that stuff!

'Really unappetising,' thought Blueskin who was developing a taste for fresh, brown rodents that cracked in his mouth like hard biscuits.

Although he didn't care for any of it, if he had to he would get used to shipboard life. Blueskin arrived on deck in time to see the first kegs of beer being stowed below. There would be ten thousand pints stored before the day was out. He licked his lips. After he had dealt with Anthony and John he would be able to enjoy himself on that little lot quite comfortably. The only flaw in his plan was that he would end up in the Americas. That might not be a bad idea, after all why stay in a country that's hanged you?

One of the men began to sing on the deck and the others joined him. It was a short song which they made up as they went along. They're the best because they go on for hours and you have to think about the words. And thinking about the words takes your mind off your tired arms and legs.

   ♪   Move down, Heave down,
         Lay down, Stay down,
      Lie down, Keep down,
     Roll down, Go down,
        Blue cat, Heave down,
       Good luck, Slow down,   ♪

Came their voices each one pulling at a large rope on every 'heave' and getting the cannons into place on the gun deck which was below the upper-deck. Pirates had sunk seven vessels in the passed month alone.

Blueskin wandered over his ship. He eyed the complex rigging of the three masts; mizzen, main and fore, and the bowsprit. The bowsprit stuck out from the front end of the galleon and anyone on it would be above the water. If they fell in they would be engulfed beneath the hull.

'There's a chance there' he thought looking at the water. 'But how could I get them onto it?'

He looked at the rigging and saw how simple it would be to get entangled in the ratlines, step on a cat at the wrong moment at the wrong height and down they would come.

He smelled the cannon which would be loaded when they entered dangerous waters ready to fire within an hour of sighting another vessel which might be hostile. Plenty of opportunity to fit a prime wire and light it whilst Matilda and Anthony were canoodling.

'She isn't really my enemy but ... well she shouldn't be stuck on Anthony. I can't help it if she gets hurt.'

His whiskers twitched. He scratched. He licked his paws. He didn't like being dirty. He had never cared about being dirty before but now, he didn't like it at all. He spent several minutes every half-an-hour

He tested the hold, scratched at the halyards which

moved the sails up and down on their yards. He sniffed into every hold, crack and room aboard.

John came down from the captain and shook his hand.

"That's settled then. I'll navigate the waters for you. We'll be here Tuesday morning." He walked off and Blueskin jumped down and followed him.

"Seen the ship have you?" said John. "I'll bet you even plan to come along with us!" Blueskin purred. "Devil take it I think you understand what I'm saying!"

They had to wait two days longer before fair winds swept through the town and out to sea. Men sprang up the rigging and the anchor was slowly hauled in. They were leaving to catch the wind whilst it was with them. It was just as well Anthony, John and Matilda has decided to stow their belongings on the day before otherwise they might have missed the boat. It was even better for Blueskin that he had decided to stick with them and not go hunting with a ginger-tom he had met in the town who used to be a member of the House of Lords, because he would certainly have missed it.

The galleon was pulled backwards until it floated above the anchor which finally pulled free off the bottom, "Anchor Away!" Called a seaman. Blueskin stretched from beneath the ship's stairs on the upper deck. Not a single soldier had come. Either Matilda's father had sent them to the wrong place or he didn't care for his daughter enough to get her back.

'Good job I've prepared my own plans,' he thought, 'I couldn't trust another person when I was a human and I can't now I'm a cat. Stupid old codger. What did I expect from a man who couldn't shoot straight.'

"That's it!" smiled John standing on the forecastle beside one of the smaller cannon.

Anthony gave Matilda a hug. The captain shouted for the fore sails to be lowered and the galleon turned slowly and headed out to sea. More sails were lowered as she went and a man turned her wheel to steer her free of the other ships and rocks.

Blueskin began to feel sick as the galleon was gently brought windward. Foremast and mainmast sails filled with the breezes bending towards the New World. Well, actually it was more towards Spain as they had to get out of the Channel and into the Atlantic before they were really on the right bearing.

Blueskin was still feeling sick when Anthony passed the captain five pounds and stood the entire crew a drink of beer as, three miles out, he was married to Matilda.

"There son! That's done you," said the captain, "Now

keep quiet for the rest of the voyage!"

"Aye! Aye!" whooped Anthony. Matilda kissed John and the captain and the crew cheered from wherever they were, except those on the ratlines and rigging who didn't particularly want to fall off.

"That's that!" said John.

"You have a sister after all!" announced Anthony.

"Ay. And Blueskin to thank for it I'm thinking," responded John thinking of the money.

This reminded him of the cat. He eyed it as it sat, curled up and innocent by the door to the cabins below.

"What are we going to call that cat? Its taken such a liking to us I don't think it will ever leave us now."

"Felix," suggested Anthony.

"Stupid name for cat."

"How about Silvester?" suggested Matilda.

"Even stupider," rejected John.

"You know, seeing how it turned up after the hanging and has that blue sheen in the sunlight I'm of the opinion we should call him Blueskin, in memory of the man who gave us enough money to start a new life."

"If you must," said John looking at him. Anthony winked at Matilda. He had told her how superstitious John was about this particular cat.

Blueskin looked up and shook his head. He was feeling too sick to make any noise. His stomach churned. The galleon rolled gently in the calm waters and it felt like a storm. He teetered on the wooden deck and tried a dignified stroll up the steps to be kicked accidentally by Anthony trying to carry Matilda to their quarters. His head swam and he lay down unable for the minute to lick his side. If he had been quicker he'd have scratched the clod-hopping oaf. Couldn't he see there was a cat in front of him! Blueskin wanted to imagine a hundred horrible punishments for him for kicking him, but all he manage to do was be sick.

The crew slept with the cannons on the gun deck in hammocks slung anywhere there was room. And there wasn't enough room to swing a cat.

Because they were newlyweds the captain gave Matilda and Anthony ship's officers' quarters. John having been an officer in the navy for six years before meeting up with Anthony and his love quest, was next door. In return John took over as chief navigator which, unlike Anthony's wedding celebration, would actually earn the three of them some money. Or should we say four of them? Blueskin having the honorary position of ship's cat, although he didn't know it when they set sail. In fact he didn't know it until he stopped being sick.

Blueskin was below the steps looking belatedly at the remains of the mouse and cockroach he had eaten an hour ago. He couldn't get over this perverted appetite. He really wanted meat and ale but whenever he was near something that moved he had this urge to take a swipe at it and chew it's head off.

'I feel very ill,' he thought.

He made his way unsteadily to the quarters and pushed open the unlocked door. Matilda and Anthony were playing cards. The last thing he wanted to see was those two enjoying themselves so he turned and left.

'If I feel like this all the way I'll never have the strength to get rid of them,' he thought. 'I wonder if the ship's doctor has any medicine.'

To call him the ship's doctor is slightly misleading. What confronted Blueskin was a thirty-five year old man who enjoyed cutting people's limbs off, polished his hatchet and five inch saw endlessly whilst waiting for someone to be brought in with a stomach ache. This man was so sadistic the sight of blood make him feel well, screams of agony made him feel like he'd been to a concert and a burial at sea only made him unhappy because he lost the right to examine a living body.

His eyes lit up at the sight of Blueskin.

"Here, kitty," he smirked from behind his beard, "I won't hurt you. Come here to kitty. Let's see how sharp our saw is eh? Nice kitty with the nice fur I could put on my pillow to keep my neck warm! Here kitty."

It was a good thing Blueskin was still able to understand English. It was also a good thing he knew enough about people to see a rotten one when they came along. His fur hackled. His teeth itched, which was a really odd feeling.

"We could try the odd experiment or two," suggested the doctor, "See how you get along with three feet, then two, then one, or how long you can swim without drowning. Here Kitty!"

The man made a quick move but Blueskin had been watching him. He wasn't so ill that he couldn't move quickly. He fled from the room and out of the doctor's reach and up the steps to the gun-deck in a blinding flash of blue. The doctor tried to follow him but somehow he didn't like leaving his room. Outside it he didn't feel in control and he had to be quite pleasant to everyone because none of the men trusted him. Inside his room he was a demon!

'Nice kitty! Stupid idiot. I'll have to watch that one,' complained Blueskin to no one in particular as he caught his breath beside a small stack of cannon balls. He still felt more at home next to weapons than anywhere else but he found it very frustrating not to be able to use any of them.

The gun-deck was filled with men resting, tidying up their few possessions and making sure the ropes were secure. If a cannon broke loose it killed and maimed because they rolled on their wheels and were very heavy. Which was a good reason why Blueskin was upset that Anthony and John were not to sleep here. Suddenly a thick-set man walked up to one of the sailors and rapped a cannon with his stick.

"Waites why isn't this gun clean?" He cried. "This should shine! Shine. I want it shining! If any of those pirates get to us I want them dazzled by the brilliance of this cannon before they can fire a single shot understand!"

The shout from officer Crank made everyone stand up, if they could, and everyone started spitting and polishing the cannon and falling over themselves to look busy.

The man who did the shouting saw Blueskin, who also happened to look rested.

"Ship's cat get the rats and get off my deck!" he shouted.

He aimed a kick at Blueskin who deftly jumped and let the man kick the cannon balls he had been lying beside. In the dimness of the gun-deck it had looked like part of him. The officer yelled black-and-blue words that cannot be repeated, and several of the crew hid their smirks. They remembered what they saw and from that day often tried the trick on new seamen giving not a few of them broken toes! It was an initiation Blueskin the highwayman would have appreciated and one which Blueskin the cat was proud to have invented even if he had been sea-sick at the time.

Blueskin raced up the deck to get away from Crank. He found a convenient damp recess. Although he had a new enemy in officer Crank from now on the crew would be well disposed towards him. Unfortunately they were all kept so busy none of them had any time to stroke Blueskin. Which he probably wouldn't have enjoyed because none of them were very clean and he had enough trouble keeping dirt off his fur without them messing it up.

Crank was limping on that foot for two days and he could never show his face that some of the men huddled together to hide their laughter. Crank never ceased to give Blueskin the most deathly of looks because of that! Even when Blueskin left a large rat on the floor outside his door it didn't change him.

And that wasn't the end of Blueskin's problems. Curled up on Matilda's lap having his stomach stroked every morning and afternoon brought out his new cat-instincts. He liked to be warm. He liked to be stroked.

Blueskin was becoming a companion animal!

One-Eyed Tim

The Pirates

"I can't see that much," moaned the first mate looking aft, scanning the gloom of early morning.

"Maybe you can't but I can smell 'em," responded the second mate. Another man had climbed into the crows nest and peered into the distance through the mist.

As the sun began to rise the sea slowly revealed its shapes and secrets, the cut of another vessel came into focus.

"SHIP AHOY!" shouted the lookout from the crows nest pointing excitedly. The men all ran to the sides of the ship to look back to see.

"There! No more than a hour behind!"

"Snuck up on us during the night. A bit faster and they would have been broadside by now blowing us to smithereens," spat the first mate.

"That's one-eyed Tim's ship that is," shouted another man. The name of the pirate captain was whispered amongst all the men until everyone knew who they were trying to escape.

"Best get the captain," said the second mate.

Blueskin stretched comfortably in his barrel filled with fresh straw from the animals den which he had stolen to make a bed. It kept the breeze off and left him to doze in peace when he wasn't wrapped in the folds of Matilda's dresses.

He rose and climbed out to see the rest of the crew being woken smartly and called to arms. Men were shouting orders, others appeared strapping swords to their belts and grabbing muskets from the gunnery. Anthony and Matilda didn't appear but then they hadn't been seen by the crew for a fortnight. The captain called it a honeymoon but the first mate called it a crying shame to waste a lovely wench on an fool like that. Blueskin the highwayman would have agreed with him but Blueskin the cat didn't take the comment lightly. If they were in a dangerous position he wanted to know all about it. After all now he liked her he didn't want Matilda being killed.

John meanwhile had worked hard at his duties. It was he who had first seen the pirate ship approaching the evening before. He had been taking a few late readings for their course correction. Men had kept watch all night in case he was right and now they all knew he was. Several of them had been detailed to prepare all arms by candlelight and it took only a few minutes for everything to be ready for battle.

The skull-and-crossbones waved in the growing breeze like an unwelcome visitor visible through a glass front door. The pirates had been having a good season but this particular crew hadn't seen a ship for nearly ten days. The last one had been Dutch. After a days chase and a long battle the pirates had found only cups, saucers and plates by the thousand! When they saw the English galleon they went mad. Surely this one would have lots of valuables aboard!

"What shall we do?" John asked the captain.

"I've a hundred and forty-two passengers who want to get to the Americas in one piece. We shall try to outrun her!" He answered.

"We won't make it . She's faster," pointed out the second mate.

"Down with all the sails. Bring her to windward."

The captain looked at John.

"If we can run her into that bad weather ahead we have a chance of losing them and they knows it."

"Get up there before I flail your hides!" shouted the second mate to some of the crew.

"Move you men! Move!" ordered the first mate, "Your

lives depend upon it!"

"Starboard cannon-ports open!"

"Down with the foremain!"

"Down below. Children down below. Twenty muskets to the forecastle. Fifteen pikes to the quarterdeck."

On the gun deck the men manned each gun fitting in the priming wires. Only one torch was lit ready to set ablaze all the others with boys running down the lines when the pirate ship closed in.

"Make fast all ropes!" ordered the captain.

The ten sails finally began to fill with the freshening breeze. The galleon gathered pace but the pirate ship had been waiting and preparing for longer. She was only three-quarters of an hour behind and gaining all the time. Cutting the water like a knife. They could see the pirates now and there on the bow was one-eyed Tim. It was said he had bet his eye he would capture ten ships in a year and when he captured eleven the other pirate claimed his eye because ten is not eleven. Which is very true.

The pirate boat was slightly smaller and faster but if the galleon kept ahead for long enough they might have tired of the chase, or lost their quarry in worsening weather which the captain could see in the stormy, dark clouds ahead. In fact he had rarely seen worse.

The eight pumps worked to clear all the water from the bilges, building up her speed by making the galleon's line smoother in the water and at last with all the noise and running about Anthony stuck his head out of his window to see what was going on.

Being aft he had a clear view of the pirate ship behind them and he got a shock at the sight of it. Quick as a flash he had his trousers on and was running to his brother's side. He passed men racing with barrels to secure the food stocks and lashing down everything that might move in the attack. After all chain shot or a cannon ball might kill you but you should at least make sure the longboat doesn't move and crush you or some loose piece of wood knock you senseless.

"Anything I can do?" asked Anthony.

"Can you handle a musket man?" asked the captain?"

"Yes."

"Gun officer! Arm this man."

"Sir. Seventeen of the passengers want to be armed as well sir."

"Do we have the guns?"

"Yes sir."

"Give them to them. Get that foremain down properly!"

The order was shouted in relays until the sailors hanging

from the yards on the foremast got it and freed the halyards getting in the way of the sail.

"All sails blowing!" called the second mate.

"It's a close thing you're trying captain. If we outrun them we're only going to have a few minutes to get the sails down before we hit the storm and if we hit the storm before we outrun them we could be torn to pieces by the wind."

The captain said nothing. He knew the risks.

"We've got women to protect," he said under his breath then he said aloud, "Get the men down to the gun deck! How are the guns?"

"All ready."

"Men at arms?"

"One hundred and three."

"Keep her steady! John, how long before they catch us?"

"Perhaps half-an-hour. By the hour of nine they may be broadside."

"First mate how many guns ready to get the sails and mast?"

"Fifteen starboard sir!"

"Good. When we know how she comes put chain-shot in all the cannons. If we can bring her rigging down and fell a mast or two we might get away uninjured."

"Aye, Sir!"

Blueskin walked down the starboard side and looked at the men waiting for orders. They sat by the rigging and stood on the deck looking aft at the encroaching enemy.

'This is a dangerous place,' he thought trying to find Anthony. A few minutes later he found him on the quarterdeck ready to protect his brother John who had taken up his position there along with some of the better marksmen amongst the crew.

"Hello there, Blueskin," smiled Anthony. "Come to bring us good luck?"

'You'll need it,' purred Blueskin.

He went over to one of the muskets and tried to get his claw into the trigger. He couldn't do it.

"Even the cat wants to take a shot at the pirates," laughed one of the crew.

Blueskin shook his head sadly. What could he use as a weapon against men? Then he saw the lower of the sails on the mizzen mast. If he could get onto it maybe he could loosen the yard and have it come crashing down in the fight. If it didn't crush a couple of pirates it would make them easy targets for the crew. Blueskin had never been scared of a fight and though he still wanted his revenge on the brothers he didn't want to see the rest of crew hacked to pieces.

Blueskin was a good climber but even as a cat he found it hard to get up the rigging. The men who went up rigging to get a shot at the enemy were mostly on the mizzen mast. They seemed almost glad of a cat trying to get up with them and didn't make a fuss. Everyone was convinced that Blueskin was a good-luck charm since his trick on officer Crank. (Sailors are extremely superstitious. A fact most cats are keen to exploit.)

Blueskin slipped and clawed his way to the first yard on which the sail hanged and tried to make his way across. It wasn't easy. The ropes were made to hold heavy sails in place and they had been hardened by the salt in the sea. It has been said that the first rock ever made had 'hope' written through it because a man watched a blue cat tearing and biting at stiff roping that day when the pirates attacked Hope of the Seas. By the time the pirates attacked Blueskin was only just getting into it and trying to cut the first ropes with his claws and teeth.

The pirate's cannon fired first and then the Hope of the Seas replied.

Then no one knew.

A complete chaos of shots and chunks of iron flying hither and thither and men falling down and being carried away or left until the Hope of the Seas managed to tear into the main mast and rip the pirate sails to shreds.

The pirate vessel returned fire as a bullet narrowly missed Anthony whilst he reloaded his musket.

Men lined the sides of the pirate vessel throwing grappling hooks, firing shot, waving swords and generally looking fierce, desperate and loud.

The Hope of the Seas carried on firing in orderly fashion forty men at a time.

Blueskin put a claw onto the wood and slipped grasping the yard with his front claws and lifting his back legs up to get his balance. Another bullet almost winged his tail. 'Pirates,' her thought, 'always firing willy-nilly never aiming at anything.'

The noise around him was deafening and he didn't know how people could be so involved in such a silly activity. Being a highwayman had always been subtle, he hated chases. In fact he had only ever loaded one of his muskets, which he always fired in the air, and everyone got the message. He had known a footpad once who had three muskets stuffed in his belt, and two in the saddle bag he carried everywhere with him for the day he could afford a horse and become a highwayman. He had asked him why he wanted five muskets. "In case I ever meet any pirates," he had replied, "useless with guns that lot fire all over the place."

Nevertheless, the crews were fighting hard and he had a problem. He was directly above Anthony. He stayed there giving up trying to make the sail fall as the ropes were too many and too strong. He positioned himself for a jump. If it was going to be of any use at all it would have to be a surprise leap.

His tail flicked expectantly as the pirate vessel fired again. Hope of the Seas let rip with six cannon and the pirates were caught badly as the remnants of their torn mainsail fell to pieces on the deck. Then cannon shot took out two of the cannon on Hope of the Seas.

"Now!" ordered the captain.

A small catapult of burning coals was thrown into the pirate ship setting light to the fallen sail. Men left their stations to carry water to put it out just as another group swung over on their ropes. Blueskin waggled the back of his body and leapt, front claws extended.

In the smoke and dirt of the cannon fire which had broken wood and injured and killed men all over the galleon Anthony didn't see the first pirates swinging into action to board the ship. They were trying to get to the wheel and turn the galleon head to wind which would stop her dead in her tracks and give them time to board her and fight it out with the crew. The main force of pirates excelled at hand-to-hand fighting.

They would have succeeded as well because there were only seven men left guarding the wheel when they tried to board.

It was a crucial moment.

The moment when the battle would be won or lost.

The men had swung over when the boats were quite far apart. They only just made it onto the bulwarks along the ship's side. Three of them got a foot hold and were just letting go of their ropes. Anthony stood back, his musket empty, ready to take a few of them.

Blueskin looked at them and in that instant thought about being hanged. And how Anthony and John had roughed-him up when they caught him. Then he thought of Matilda's comfortable lap. Then he thought of his blue waistcoat and how good he looked in it. Then he thought about Matilda's lap. Then he thought about the prison and how much he had hated it. Then he thought about Matilda's lap. He didn't know whether to help Anthony or let him perish!

Then he jumped.

Blueskin had never thought about flying in his life. If he had been asked about it he would have laughed and moved on. Why it struck him that as a cat he would be able to fly he had no idea. All the knew was he had to go from where he was, downwards, so he leapt. And his leap became a fall.

Using no more than his nose to guide his leap he fixed himself to the head of the pirate in the middle. The man let go the rope, tottered backwards and shot out his arms to left and right seeking something to hold onto. Blueskin spat loudly and put his claws into the man's eyes.

The two pirates with him were also put off balance by the man's groping to get Blueskin off. Seizing the chance Anthony took his empty musket and smashed their feet making them jump and yell in pain. There was quite a bit of spitting on all sides. And more than a few scratches.

Blueskin jumped down as the pirates fell into the sea along with two others who were swinging in behind them. The sixth and seventh didn't try to let go their ropes and swung back to their own ship which was disengaging. Much of her sails were ruined and there was a roaring fire on the upper deck.

"Give them a farewell shot!" ordered the captain.

The guns along the aft rang out, most of their shot falling into the sea. The captain looked at the pirate vessel as it made off in worsening seas and at Blueskin as he did the same.

"That cat of yours is something rare," he said.

"I know. Quite a fighter," agreed Anthony.

"Saved our bacon and no mistake," said the first mate with appreciation.

"Are you alright?" called the ship's doctor.

"Eight dead here and two wounded," called back the captain. "Check all damage," he told the first mate. "And watch the doctor doesn't do more damage to the men than the pirates." The wind howled throughout the ship.

"Weather is worsening," muttered John.

"Hold breaking a barrel of rum for the men until we are through the storm," ordered the captain."

"We can't wait to celebrate," said a sailor.

"Aye, we showed them this time," agreed his mate. Thunder peeled in the distance.

Blueskin curled up with his thoughts. Anthony had left his new wife to fight with them.

'That's courage and a sense of right and wrong.' He thought. 'I never had that when I was a man. I wonder why I have it now I'm a cat?'

He licked his front paws thoughtfully. For the first time in either of his two lives he was beginning to like himself.

And he quite forgot how close he had come to not saving Anthony's life.

The
Storm

"Well?" shouted the captain over the growing howl of the wind.

"There's at least two weeks work to repair the ship, cap'n, according to the carpenter," replied his second mate. "Seventeen of our trained crew are dead in all and another six others are with the ship's doctor. So they'll be dead soon an' all. The men are right cheerful of the cat and those two you hired on well, they proved themselves alright."

"What's the weather look like?" asked Anthony. John smiled.

"Landlubber!" he said, "You've only got to look out to see what its doing!"

"It looks dark."

"That will be the clouds blocking out the sunshine."

" Will it be rough?"

"That storm we saw brewing before the pirates attacked is on the way. Seas bringing up close to the hold right now. We'll be in her come another hour."

"I'd say we could have a rough night," stated Anthony trying to sound sailor-like.

"I agree with that," said the second mate putting on a thick jacket against the cold. "we might not be in good shape to withstand a hurricane."

"Try to make up our numbers with volunteers," suggested the captain.

"What can landlubbers do?"

"Get them to clear the decks of sail and broken wood. Just throw the lot overboard this is going to be a hell of a storm and we haven't time to search for bits and pieces we could use again. Get every other man onto battening hatches and stowing sail. Get the men working. Use loose rigging as extra roping."

"Are you alright?" Anthony asked John seeing blood on his shirt.

"Slight scratch otherwise fair. How's Matilda?"

"With the others. She's helping the doctor with some of the injured. He's a funny chap. Seems to enjoy all the blood and wounds. Apparently he has taken a shine to her."

"Who doesn't."

"Looks like we're in for it?"

"The storm may well do what the pirates failed to achieve." John looked up and saw the sails beginning to strain as the wind blew harder. "There she is under the black clouds. It will be dark by the time we are in the heart of her. We might be too badly holed to get through. We've got to get prepared before its too rough to move around. "

"I'll help."

"Better not, Anthony. You're not a mariner and the only men who should be on deck have to know where to put their feet. One slip in a damaged ship in a storm could send you overboard."

'Really,' thought Blueskin who had been eavesdropping, 'in that case I had better keep my eyes open.' But although he thought it, he wasn't sure he really felt he wanted revenge as much. He had liked all the pats and strokes he had gotten for the way in which he had dealt with those pesky pirates. He liked being stroked.

The wooden masts creaked as the wind picked up and tried to snap them. Unable to spend the time clearing up properly the men threw broken wood, spars and rubbish into the sea clearing the decks of everything that could do a mischief in the oncoming storm.

Below on the gun deck they chained the cannons and plugged the cannon-ports which had been damaged. Below that in the Orlop deck they battened down everything that could move. In the hold the casks of food were secured and in the cabins trunks were hastily opened, filled with trinkets, bottles, combs and smaller items and then shut and tied to the beds which were fastened to the floors like all the furniture.

The wind blew harder. The ship began to dip and roll in the waves and water flooded through every available crack. Matilda was horrified to see the boards opening under the strain, giving her a clear view of the pirate ship floundering behind them in the heavy seas.

Which really annoyed one-eyed Tim because if there was one thing he hated more than losing a ship it was getting wet. Which is why his mother always asked him if he hated being wet so much why did he choose to be a pirate. Which is why he never visited his mother because he never had an answer for her.

Blueskin watched the men run around getting everything ready. Running up the rigging to haul in the sails. Two torn sails were lowered and taken below to be repaired. The others were rolled onto the yards as the wind picked up and the figurehead on the Hope of the Seas began to dive so deep into the waves disappearing for seconds at a time. Waves washed over the decks soaking everyone. The man in the crows nest came down with his last report on the size of the waves ahead. The storm was gathering pace very quickly.

Half an hour before she hit men were ordered down from the rigging and went below. When the ship went through the storm the top of the masts would roll so much they would touch the waves and in such conditions no man was safe. Those left on the top deck began to tie themselves to ropes which allowed them to keep their stations without being washed away. Two men were put to the wheel and others secured themselves tightly to the strongest wood. Two other men trailed a thick rope off the aft in case any were washed overboard. They could grab at it whilst it floated in the sea and save themselves. But they soon realised this was going to be a great storm and the rope wouldn't be much use. The waves would swallow anyone within seconds.

The storm rose and wailed in their ears. They could hardly see through the spray as it washed over and over, hitting the sides of the galleon until they didn't believe she could take anymore. The waves grew higher until they crashed over the galleon rocking her violently from side to side. Below, salt water gushed in. The ship strained to keep together. Masts seemed to bend and everyone was filled with the fear that the ship couldn't stay afloat. It just couldn't. They huddled into corners and hugged one another. How could they hope to survive?

Only the sailors who had been through it all before knew they might weather this storm but the passengers were first time sailors and were terrified. Another day passed and they knew they were in the middle of a storm that would take them where it wanted. Anthony grew worried. He hadn't seen John for hours. He came out to see if he could help his brother. Blueskin was wrapped up beneath the steps leading to the upper deck where he felt reasonably safe. His barrel had been blown overboard. As Anthony walked past him grabbing the railings tightly to steady his steps Blueskin knew he had to follow him. He didn't like getting wet but he knew Anthony was heading for trouble again!

"John?" shouted out Anthony.

His voice almost like a whisper in the noise and rumble. The thunder rolled in time to the galleon and lightning came streaking across the sky lighting up the inky blackness. The waves crashed over the deck and Anthony fell onto his face thrown across the deck like a rag-doll. He tried to get up sodden and blinded by sea water.

"What's that man doing down there?" Cried the captain picking out Anthony as he fought to get to them.

"It's one of the passengers. No tar would be fool enough to be down there in this."

"I'll get him," cried John preparing to untie his roping.

"Nay! Stay here. That's an order."

"But captain…"

"An Order I say! Let one fool be thrown overboard in this storm but two I'll not lose! You're a navigator. Without you not just one but all of us may perish"

Blueskin made his way across the deck by digging his claws into the wood softened by the water. At one side he reached a rope and began to bite at the loose knot pulling it through until the rope went limp. It was exactly opposite to where Anthony was holding on for dear life screaming at the top of his voice without being heard. Anthony wasn't tied to anything as he had tried to clamber over the hatches to find John and help. He at last managed to stand up at just the wrong time. A wave crashed into the side of the ship, she rolled and Anthony was in the water. Blueskin gripped the end of the rope and like a feline Tarzan swung across the width of the deck.

It has been said that a man could be thrown into the sea by one wave and tossed back onto the boat by the next. Anthony was tossed high, left the boat completely, raised his arms in fright and was hit by the rope and Blueskin as they swung in. He grabbed at it and came swinging back into the shrouds where he hanged for dear life whilst being ducked into the water by the rolling and pitching of the boat.

"Captain," called the first mate, "I think he's alright."

"Damn the fool. Keep your stations. If he lives he would have learned a lesson."

Meanwhile Blueskin was in trouble having been grabbed by a wet and cold Anthony and nearly drowned in the ferocious waters of the ocean. "What are you doing here?" Anthony bellowed into the cat's ear.

'I could ask you the same question,' moaned Blueskin to himself having all the breath squeezed out of him by Anthony's strong grasp.

"Come on. This is no place for the likes of us."

'I'm not so sure,' thought Blueskin, 'After all if the galleon goes down at least we'll be holding onto something whilst if we. . .'

He didn't finish. He was unceremoniously stuffed into a soaking wet jacket which was then buttoned, with difficulty over him. He felt like scratching Anthony but thought better of it. At least he was warm. Even if the idiot was still alive. Truth to tell Blueskin had been in two minds as the rope sailed across the deck. Half of him wanted to save Anthony and half wanted to give him an extra push to make sure he drowned.

John had watched this with interest. He couldn't make out what the man had caught. He couldn't even make out the man was his brother. But he was more interested in what was going on than in the storm. Or maybe what was going on helped calm his nerves. He for one didn't think they were going to make it. He could already see the rigging tearing up, the halyards giving way. It would only take a mast to fall in this storm to hole them badly.

Anthony grabbed at the rigging and put his head under his arm. The salt water burned as it touched his skin so cold and forceful was its strength. He pulled himself down the rigging spending most of the time in the water and staggered over the bulwark being thrown onto his back and squashing Blueskin on his way back to the stairs which he grabbed tightly. Making the entrance hatch to the cabin below he stumbled in followed by gallons of water.

It took nearly half-an-hour but he made it and was hauled in by a man who was watching. The wet and tired Anthony was carried down into the cabin where Matilda began to undo his coat and screamed when a half dead cat was found almost stuck to her husband's shirt. One of the women took the animal up and put it onto the pillow on the chair just as the ship lurched once more and sent them flying.

Blueskin had horrible dreams about drowning and being sick. Of a soft pillow and gentle hands. Then of a huge wave and a cracking and creaking and shouts and screams and masts collapsing and boats being hauled into the sea. When he woke up he was tired, hungry and cold and tied to the chair. He briefly thought it was a rotten trick and pulled wildly at the string until he was free and on the beach.

He stood up and promptly lost the feeling in his legs. Someone had tied him onto this wood and he was angry. The connections between a storm and a beach are obvious to those of you who are reading, comfortably snuggled on a chair or lying on a bed but to a cat who had unknowingly come through a shipwreck after being mauled by Anthony and half-drowned, the connection was slow. Very slow. Blueskin sat down and looked out to sea. Nothing. He turned and looked at the broken chair which had brought him to the safety on what appeared to be an island. It slowly dawned on him that being tied to a chair was a clue. He stood up and shook himself. He realised what had happened. Bits of debris were washed ashore by each wavelet. Amongst them pieces from the Hope of the Seas.

'I wonder if they all drowned,' was his first thought. 'I wouldn't mind if Crank was' he added to himself. 'I wonder where this is. It can't be the famous Americas we weren't at sea long enough to get close. Maybe we're in Ireland. I hear that's a fun place to be. Or maybe this is just an island with no one around and I'll have to live here for the rest of my life. Well that's only a few years. After all I'm a cat not a man.'

He got up slowly and licked his salty feet. He shook himself and began to walk across the sand. He felt the fine grains give gently beneath his paws. He suddenly realised how much he had missed dry land in the weeks he had been at sea. As he walked across the beach he came to a line of rocks. And as he climbed them he found he had an elevated view of the beach ahead. And as he peered down he saw something that made his whole body flood with amazement.

Large as life and sitting up was Anthony. Was John. Was Matilda. No one else. Sitting by one of the life-boats from the Hope of the Seas.

'Even a shipwreck can't kill those two,' he thought!

Hope of the Seas finds land the hard way

The Shipwrecked

Blueskin was nothing if not cat-resilient. He joined them by the longboat which they had scrambled into during the height of the storm. They had lost its oars, and there were no provisions in its storage holds.

"Well look at this!" smiled a damp Matilda at the sight of Blueskin. Whenever the three of them thought of Blueskin it was as a lifesaver and lucky mascot. The other survivors looked up. Anthony had told him about the rope and John actually felt like trusting the cat now!

"That cat's had most of its nine lives."
As Blueskin walked down Anthony got up,
"There's more to this cat than meets the eye, John. It's saved my life thrice. Once with Matilda's father, once with those pirates and again last night, just before Hope of the Seas broke and we manned the lifeboat. I aint a man for such things but I think that cat was meant to be with us."

"That's no ordinary cat, I agree."

"Aye, that may well be," said one of the sailors sitting up in the boat which he had been cleaning out. "They say some animals are the souls of the dead."

"Anthony tells me that's what you said," Matilda mentioned looking at John.

"I did, and well, maybe, in a way I was right. But I can't say I knew the right person. See, Blueskin had been hanged less than a hour when he turned up at Anthony's feet and I saw the blue in its coat...turned me cold. But I reckon this cat must have been some ministering angel, parson or saint"

"Would that Blueskin be the highwayman hanged at the assizes 'fore we put to sea?" asked the sailor recognizing the name.

"The same," said Anthony.

"Some job getting that one to the rope," spat the sailor.

"But this can't be Blueskin. He'd be mad at us. He'd rather try to kill us than save our lives," answered John.

Never was a truer word uttered in ignorance. Blueskin licked his front, left paw. He suddenly felt guilty. Something he had never felt before. For a few seconds he mistook it for being hungry. Then he thought it might be wind. But he realised it must be guilt because he had a lump in his throat that wasn't fur.

"I'll wager you've been reading the signs wrong," said the sailor getting out of the boat and sitting on the side. He held a net in his hand ready to try some fishing close to shore to get something for them to eat.

"No! He got Matilda's father just as he was about to shoot at us. He fell on that pirate just as he would have carved me in twain. He loosed that rope just as I was washed overboard. I'm telling you I think he's some kind of God's angel come to look after us," Anthony stroked the cat as it passed him. Blueskin purred.

"He wasn't around when we caught the real Blueskin. That's when we needed him most," argued John.

"He wasn't around when we were born. That's not for us to comment on. The spirits send their gifts as and when they want to. He's here now." Anthony got up and gave Blueskin a long stroke along his back.

"Try to get some fish for his supper," he asked the sailor.

"If the others can't find anything on this island I'll 'ave enough doing to get food for us without bothering over a cat that should 'ave drowned with the rest of 'em."

"You can always try," asked Anthony.

"So could you if you're so fond of the damnable animal!"

The sailor looked at the cat. It was the same look Blueskin remembered from the town the first time he had met

Anthony. The look which said if I don't find any fish you'll feed three or four of us yourself! The sailor left to walk into the sea until it was up to his hips. He cast the net wide and watched as it dredged up a crab or two on the bottom.

Blueskin wondered how long the others would be and if they would have success in finding food. He was going to stick close to Anthony and John safe in the knowledge that if anyone did try to kill him the brothers would give him a chance to get away. He yawned. He was tired. He walked away from the boat and curled up on the rocks warmed by the rising sun. He would have to keep one eye open for the sailor if he wasn't to end up food. All the talk about angels made him wonder if there was some purpose to his being a cat. Maybe he had been drawn here for a reason he didn't know about yet. It was possible.

The idea thrilled him and he sniffed the air keenly as he sank into sleepiness. There were new places to explore. Who knows what there was to find here. He suddenly thought of the dangers. There were wild animals, even a cannibal or two. Who knew? It wouldn't be any good trying to strike out on his own yet, he needed to know more about the place! He didn't know they were in California. They had been blown them from sea to another. That was some storm!

He awoke and smelled a fire and peeped over the rocks.

There on the beach the nineteen remaining of the crew and passengers of the Hope of the Seas were eating fish and birds caught by the party who went inland. They had found water a league away and come back to haul the boat well out of the sea and eat. Matilda sat on the boat looking at the evening stars when she felt a warm, furry animal at her feet.

Blueskin sat beside her and contentedly let her feed him. He remembered the days when women would feed him for fun at Filyrank's tavern and he would kiss them and they would laugh when he showed them the latest bauble he had stolen from some noble.

"So its probably a very large island," said the second mate munching at some meat.

"Well," said John as the second mate concluded his story of what they had seen from the top of cliffs, "I haven't any idea where we are and we can't expect another ship to come along quickly. I suggest we pack up and march inland and see where we come out. From what you say chances are it might be part of a larger land. We might be in the Americas for all we know, hundreds of miles off our course. We must try to find any people who may be able to help. If it isn't the Americas we may have come to some unknown country where we could live if we've a mind."

"But we've only got the two pistols and three swords with us and no muskets. That doesn't sound good odds to go exploring," argued one of the men.

"You want to spend months here trying to get fish and wondering where we are?" asked the second mate. The sailor grunted.

"Right then. Let's pack up in the morning and start out. Wherever we are there aren't any ships coming along in a hurry, as John says, so we might as well explore."

"How about checking the beach for any other survivors?" Asked Matilda.

"All you're going to find are dead bodies," said the second mate. "We only made it because we were in a boat."

"That's true. I doubt anyone could have made it other than us," said one of the men. John nodded.

"Best concern ourselves with the living."

The group laid themselves out on the ground. They didn't need blankets it was so warm which made John think they may have been blown way west in the storm and come to some place near the equator. That's where it grew warmer and certainly it was warm enough here. This time of year New Amsterdam was in the midst of autumn but the trees here were thick and covered in leaves. The stars were littered across the sky as if strewn by some untidy tramp on his wanderings. Blueskin gave a small cat snore and dreamt for the best part of an hour about Anthony, John and Matilda living in a tree house!

They all slept well with one guard changing every four hours. The camp was quiet except Blueskin kept one eye open as he rested on the boat under Matilda's dress with his head peeping from its folds. He was the only one to see the bushes rustle and a half-naked man appear. He was tall and obviously interested by the men on the beach but wary of the guard seeing him. He crept slowly round and Blueskin watched as his spear was picked out by the light from the stars. Then the man disappeared. 'Counting them,' thought Blueskin. 'And going to tell his tribe about the travellers on the beach.' Blueskin closed both his eyes. 'Now all it needs is for them to be hostile and I'll be one busy cat. As long as they don't kill me as well.'

Losing all your friends and over two hundred people in a storm isn't exactly what you want to remember in the morning so they packed up quickly and claimed the land they had landed on for the King of England and marched inland in single file. Blueskin decided to make use of his esteem with John and Anthony and hitched a ride in Anthony's pouch bag which was slung on the man's shoulder. From here he kept an eye and ear open and alert for other men. To begin with they retraced the steps of the exploration the day before and arrived at the top of the cliffs and looked out towards to sea. There was no sign of other boats and the beach was empty in both directions for many leagues. "Just as well we didn't waste time trying to search for others," said a sailor.

John stared across and looked at a wisp of smoke rising gently upward seven miles away as the crow flew. The others saw it too.

"Could that be others from the Hope of the Seas?"

"Nay," said the second mate,"That's nowhere near any water. I'll wager that's some native people."

"Should we head that way?" asked John.

"There's two things we might find," said one of the men, "food and help or a fight. Since we're alone here it won't do no harm to try and find people who know the place. And if there's a fight we'll go down well accounted." This was his way of saying they would kill a good many before they were beaten.

"Aye, but they don't speak English," pointed out one of the others, "So how can they help us?"

"I've been told natives are hostile and ugly and not to be trusted."

"I hear tell of gentle ones who give you their wives for

the night as a sign of friendship." This brought a smatter of laughter from the men and blushes to Matilda's face. "If we go with loaded pistols we might be safe. My brother told me they don't like the gun and fear those who wield it."

"If we go we shall go in peace," said the second mate. "The gun is fashioned in evil and there should be no room for it in the New World."

"That's fancy talk," said one of the sailors, "I don't see it would 'ave 'elped much 'gainst those pirates."

They argued for a while longer but no one put up serious objections to going through the forest to find who was making the smoke. They would only shoot if attacked.

It was a long walk and Blueskin kept a sharp look out. As it was he was sure they were being flanked by at least six men but he was worried they made no move against them. He guessed they were waiting for reinforcements to arrive before attacking. Fortunately he was wrong. What they were waiting for was to see where the men were going and what they were doing. Since they walked in good order, talked as they went and didn't seem hostile the Indians were inclined to watch and do nothing. By that afternoon they had walked fifteen miles and Matilda was exhausted. So was Blueskin who had found bouncing around in Anthony's pouch uncomfortable and almost as bad as being on a ship. When they sat down in a clearing for the third rest of the day the six Washo American Indians (for that is who they were) suddenly appeared. John stood up and one of the men took out his pistol.

"No need of that," said John. "Let's see if they are friendly." He walked over with two sailors beside him ready to draw their cutlasses. John nodded at the Washo and smiled. Smiling is one of the few facial movements recognizable by all people and the Washo nodded back. One of them held out a hand and pointed westward. "Do you think he wants to take us somewhere?" asked one of the sailors.

"He might do," agreed John. "Do we have any objections?"

"None," they chorused.

They got up and fell in behind the Washo who led the way through the forest and out to where three more of their tribe were waiting on the edge of a great plain which stretched as far as the eye could see. Here they had twenty-eight unshod horses lightly covered with a blanket wearing no reins or stirrups. "Well, well. They've brought us transport," said Anthony.

"A sure sign they want to help," said Matilda.

'So that's why they counted us,' thought Blueskin. The men all mounted a horse each although few of them could ride. These were fine, healthy horses newly broken and much prized by the Washo. One or two bucked a bit but only one sailor fell off much to their amusement. They started off at a walk following unseen trails and wondering were the Washo were taking them.

Then they met up with the main body of men. They talked hurriedly after greeting each other. The newly arrived tribesmen talked and nodded at the travellers. They were carrying dead buffalo cut up and stored on their pack horses ready for a feast at the camp. The hides neatly wrapped into bundles. They had never expected their comrades to have such a haul as nineteen strange people who had come out of the sea after the storm. There were obviously some good, tall tales to be got out of this at the feast that was going to be held in their camp to celebrate the finest buffalo hunt of the year.

The Medicine-Man

They were everywhere. They were well kept. They were clean. They wagged their tails. They had brown and white patches. They made an awful racket and Blueskin didn't like them. They were a problem.

Blueskin leapt out of the pouch as the dogs caught his scent. He ran across the camp site and tore onto a roof for his dear life. Three of them began yelping and barking at the base wagging their tails. Others soon followed. This was their idea of fun. The last thing Blueskin needed was a pack of dogs trying to eat his tail. Hadn't it been bad enough keeping up with John and Anthony without being chased by dogs and laughed at by people who didn't even speak English.

He spat at them!

"Well they seem right friendly," said one of the sailors not in the slightest interested whether Blueskin was torn to pieces or not.

"Aye, that they do. Though I can't say I care much for

these horses. Don't see 'ow gentle-folk manage to get used to them. My bum aches awful."

"It's something you have to brought up with," suggested the second-mate.

"Just practice," said John slipping down with no problem.

"Let's share some of that food we caught. That might show our good intentions."

"It might at that. Though I can see they've got satchels of meat and all we have are a few stale fish. And not large ones either."

"Let's ask them how far we are away from New Amsterdam where we was suppose to be going," suggested another.

"Can't well ask a man a thing if you can't understand 'im," explained yet another.

"True enough," said Anthony.

"Still even if we can't get any news, we can still enjoy ourselves," commented the second mate. "Almost worth coming through a storm for!"

'Why don't they stop jawing and get me down!' Thought an outraged and very stuck Blueskin. Matilda finally walked over and tried to get through the children who were busy throwing sticks at Blueskin to see what would happen when he fell. A few mothers appeared and ran to bring them away. After all the cat was the companion of the strangers who were guests. You know how you don't upset your guests if you can help it. The dogs were also pulled off and to keep them quiet given their dinner early. Blueskin hanged onto Matilda's arms and refused to get down until no dogs were within sight. His ears were back and his tail flicked feverishly. He was angry and fed up with being a cat. But there was no changing it, he was a cat. And he rather felt he liked Matilda.

The camp was situated in the open with the forest way away in the distance. The tribe had set up there a week ago having followed the buffalo herd three hundred miles. (Although none of them would have said as much. They didn't like to boast.)

They had followed the herd for two months. Two full moons. Not that John and the others knew that. Because John and the others couldn't speak to the Washo. The Washo had never seen a white man before (or woman) and they didn't speak a single word of anything but their own language and that of a few of their neighbouring tribes. It made conversation impossible except for a few drawings. There is the sun. This is a mountain. There is the forest. "Look, that's a river and that must be the shoreline."

"What are those stick-like things?"

"That's us! That must be the part of the coast where we

landed!"

"It's a map."

"That looks like a horse."

"That's no bit of coastline I've ever seen."

"So we 're lost."

"Knew that before he started drawing the silly thing!"

"We must be far down the coast of the Americas. In a place unknown to others!"

"And which way do we go to get to New Amsterdam!"

"Who knows," shrugged John ending the speculation.

This was the gist of the their first communication with the Washo.

Things got really friendly when the tribal elders took out the peace pipe that evening stuffed with hashish and gave everyone a smoke. It made Matilda sick and Blueskin felt queasy at the smell but the tribesmen seemed to enjoy it and Anthony was soon away.

When the feasting was winding down and most of the men had turned in to get some sleep and the fires burnt low Blueskin took the night off and began his prowl with a strange voice calling him. Was this the famous call of the wild he had heard so much about?

After the first six wooden houses he realised horses were just about as good at cat-bating as dogs. It would only have taken a couple of geese and he wouldn't have been able to wink without something making a noise. It wasn't as if he was harmful to them! Maybe they heard the voice as well and wanted to get up and follow its call but couldn't so they whinnied a bit instead.

Maybe they had been people. Reincarnated Washo. Blueskin sniffed the remnants of supper and took a piece of meat from an unwashed pottery bowl. He sat down and scratched his ear trying to get the voice out of his head. Worst of all although it drew him along he didn't have the faintest idea what it was saying to him!

He heard the snores of the sailors across the quiet camp and noted what silent sleepers Washo men and women were. Not even their babies made a sound.

'Have you found what you are looking for?' Blueskin jumped and peered into dark. A man was sitting there with his legs crossed staring at him. He had red and yellow feathers in his hair, yellow paint on his face and the gnarled hands of an old man. It was the same voice that he had heard in his head.

'I think I have,' replied Blueskin. The Washo medicine man (that's a kind of clever priest who knows how to talk to spirits which live in animals and plants) nodded. 'What has driven you to our shores wild spirit?'

'You wouldn't understand,' suggested Blueskin.

'Am I not the best judge of what I do and do not understand,' responded the Medicine man.

'Probably,' agreed Blueskin.

'Then speak with me a while. I have called you for a purpose.'

'Why?'

'You floated over the great seas with the white skinned people?'

'Yes,' replied Blueskin.

'I would learn of their ways and practices and whether you come in peace or to harm us.

'I'm just a cat. Why not ask one of the others?'

'I sense you are more than a cat,' the Medicine man revealed.

'You're a clever man,' congratulated Blueskin.

He lay down and put his head between his front paws.

'You're the first person I have been able to talk to in weeks.'

'I speak to all animals willing to speak to me,' replied the old Medicine man. He took a knife and Blueskin jumped up suddenly fearful of his intentions. The man cut a slither of meat from a chunk on a plate and gave it to Blueskin,

'You are still hungry.'

'You have great magic' breathed Blueskin with his mouth full.

'What drives you to this place amongst all others?'

'It began in England a country in Europe, weeks ago. Two of those men in the party back there caught me and had me hanged.'

'This is not good. This is not good at all. Why did they have you hanged?'

'Well, it wasn't them exactly. They just caught me. It was the law which hanged me.'

'The law of one's land is there for all. Why did it not serve in your favour?'

'I…well I robbed a few people and the law said it was wrong and I…have to admit I did kill a man.'

'For this you were hanged?'

'Yes. Then I found myself as the cat you now see and I followed those men at first in the hope of getting my revenge.'

'Does that man you killed seek revenge of you as you do of the two men who caught you?' This Medicine man was sharp as a razor.

'He might.' Blueskin was caught off-guard by the question.

'But they only wanted the money for capturing me so they could come here and one of them could get married.'

'To come to our land to bring up a family is a fine thing. With this I am happy.'

'Although they almost didn't make it,' purred Blueskin.

'You have helped them?'

'I saved Anthony's life when we were attacked by pirates and again in the storm.'

'I do not know what pirates are.'

'They are sailors on the seas who attack and rob other sailors.'

'The way you robbed when you were a man?' Blueskin winced.

He didn't like to think about it but the Medicine man was right, he had been just like the pirates.

'I make a better cat than I did a man,' Blueskin said sadly.

'And so we come back to you,' concluded the Medicine man. 'What are you doing here?'

'I have told you.'

'No, all things have a reason. You have not come here by accident. I feel there is a mission for you.'

'A mission? What do you mean?'

'I mean that a cat that can think like a person can be of

great use in this country. I see many others coming here and many battles will be fought. Not by John and Anthony (he knew their names although Blueskin hadn't mentioned them) but by others who will follow them.'

'And you think I can help you with that? I have to warn you I can't even untie a rope. I know, I've tried.'

'No. The battles that are coming are ours to fight, not yours.

You have your own.'

'Where?'

'You must go and find out, far into the mountains of our tribal lands.'

'This is silly. I have just found a nice place to live and you want me to chuck it all in and go off into some freezing mountains looking for something I know nothing about.'

'It is not I. It is fate. I called you here to talk to me. But another voice will come to you and it will not rest until you have answered it. You will be driven from here into the City of the Cats.'

'What?'

'Ancient tales tell of the City of the Cats. I know little about it but you have been brought here to find and guard it. Perhaps to save it. I know not. But of all the lands in the world no one else knows of such a place. This is your fate,

Blueskin.'

'That's a lot of nonsense.'

'I shall prove it to you.'

'Go ahead.'

'Here, this is a poison. Go to your friends and place it in the food bowls, when they next eat it will kill them. Take your revenge.'

Blueskin looked at the small cube with its soft putty-like texture the Medicine man offered him. A few days ago he'd have taken it at once. But not now. He sat on his back and sniffed at it.

'My days of killing people are over,' he said. 'They have shown me kindness and they…believe me their friend. I don't want to harm them or prove them wrong.'

'This I knew,' said the Medicine man, 'But you did not. Revenge brought you here but now you have changed. Now other things will drive you.'

The Medicine man stopped talking and Blueskin felt as if he were walking on air when he left him and certain that no dog could ever harm him.

Blueskin had never had a brother. He looked down at John and Anthony. They were resting. They had arrived in their New World. They had a life ahead of them filled with adventures if they wanted them. Blueskin remembered how Anthony had petted him. How they had cared for him as a cat. How they tried to protect each other. He had always had to protect himself even as a child. He had never tried to protect anyone before. It felt...good.

He licked their hands, turned and walked across the camp. The whole of America lay in front of him. A vast, unknown territory filled with excitement. It was Blueskin's kind of country. He walked out and carried on walking into the darkness a shimmering blue light beneath the stars searching for the City of the Cats.

Blueskin was going trailblazing. . .

The

beginning

of

Little Wolf

Information on all FootSteps Press Books may be found at:

www.footsteps.co

Available from Amazon, Barnes & Noble and other outlets

FARMER FISHER: 1976 Children's Book of the Year. A delightful and tuneful picture book richly illustrated by the author. The music is available for free download from www.footsteps.co.

Farmer Fisher had a Fine Fat Truck
you couldn't see the colour for
the farmyard muck.
In the front was a Rabbit
and a Chicken and a Duck
On the way to market

BY JONATHON COUDRILLE

7+

THE EXALTED GATE: Ten traditional fairy tales with just a touch of the modern in them, inspired by the beautiful and inventive paintings of Annie Ovenden.
Share the adventure of the actress Judith who hates shoes and her magical, unwanted boots; listen to the wise dog Kai in ancient Japan; find out if Lonia will   ever get married and what made Densus turn   blue;   witness   a

dragon's last hours; discover what made Alice's granddaughter angry and how Ned saved his home. Can the elf Opikle Dinn save Rebecca's life? What can a ghost do to save Dinhama's village in ancient India? What happened when Keith learned his dog could talk?

7+

BY DANIEL NANAVATI & ANNIE OVENDEN

Lightning Source UK Ltd.
Milton Keynes UK
UKIC01n0700171013
219218UK00004B

9 780956 634931